Stop Flunking!

A Guide for Parents

How to Motivate Your Child to Get A's in School

by

Gary Bracey and Ayele Shakur

Llumina Press

© 2007 Ayele Shakur and Gary Bracey

All rights reserved. No part of this publication may be reproduced or transmitted in any form or by any means electronic or mechanical, including photocopy, recording, or any information storage and retrieval system, without permission in writing from both the copyright owner and the publisher.

Requests for permission to make copies of any part of this work should be mailed to Permissions Department, Llumina Press, PO Box 772246, Coral Springs, FL 33077-2246

ISBN: 978-1-59526-828-0

Printed in the United States of America by Llumina Press

Library of Congress Control Number: 2007904260

Dedication

This book is dedicated to our parents,
Salim & Carolyn Shakur and William & Louise Bracey,
for their love, inspiration, and encouragement;
and to the hundreds of parents who have entrusted us with helping their
children make it to the top in school.

To the Reader

This book is intended to help parents who are struggling with a child who is bright but unmotivated, and settling for failing or mediocre grades. Although the book is written specifically for parents of teenagers between the ages of 13 to 18 years old, the advice, tips, and strategies are helpful for students of all ages.

There are many things that students can do to become more successful in school, and these strategies are taught in our seminars and workshops held all across the country. But students cannot do it alone. They need the adults in their lives – their parents, family members, community workers, and teachers – to also play a role in their academic motivation.

As a parent, you can help your child develop a winning attitude for school success. We suggest you read this book all the way through from cover to cover. Then go back and highlight the sections that you want to make sure you implement right away.

We look forward to hearing your success stories!

Best wishes,
Ayele and Gary

Acknowledgements

The BIFF Paradigm Project: A Motivational Learning Skills Program was founded by Ayele Shakur and Gary Bracey, but our work would not be possible without the help of countless individuals, schools, corporations, and foundations. We would like to take this opportunity to thank the many funders who have supported our work over the years, including the Nellie Mae Education Foundation, The Boston Foundation, Black Ministerial Alliance of Greater Boston, Bank of America, State Street Foundation, the Clippership Foundation, the Dolphin Trust, Edvestors, the Harbus Foundation at Harvard Business School, the Hyams Foundation, Pierce Charitable Trust, Schrafft Charitable Trust, Nonprofit Finance Fund, the Paul and Edith Babson Foundation, the City of Boston, and hundreds of individual donors.

We also want to thank Doug Lemov at the Academy of the Pacific Rim and Audrey Leung-Tatt at the Martin Luther King Jr. Middle School for being innovative principals who believed in the dream of BIFF and allowed us to launch the BIFF Program there back in 1999. Thank you to all of the principals and school administrators who have supported our work over the years, including Myrtlene Mayfield, Spencer Blasdale, Richard Salmon, Crystal Haynes, Kevin Andrews, Brett Peiser, Jose Vidot, Mary Skipper, Ami Capodanno, Jane King, Roger Harris, James Watson, Willette Charles, Sandra McIntosh, Ipyana Wasret, Roosevelt Smith, and Yolanda Minor-Beech who brought BIFF into their schools.

Along with our partner schools, we have many agencies and institutions to thank including the Boston Public Schools, ABCD Summerworks, Jack and Jill of America, Boston Centers for Youth and

Families, the Department of Health and Human Services/Compassion Capital Fund, the Department of Housing and Urban Development, and the Massachusetts Department of Education.

We owe a debt of gratitude to countless individuals. Thank you to Steve Tritman for his endless advice and support, along with Peter Terry, Gilouse Vincent, Pierre Bois Aubin, Stacey Mednick, Violet Burch, City Councilor Chuck Turner, Vusama Kariba, Janine Burrell, Catherine Gill, Jay Sherwin, Blenda Wilson, George McCully, Terri Spoon, Petter Etholm, Tom Gee, Mamie Canton, Catherine Kostecki, Joy Lucas, Lou Casagrande, Ellen Bass, Pat Bonner-Duvall, Richard Ward, Bob Wadsworth, Sylvia Johnson, Una Kelley, Monica Roberts, Pat Burns, plus Harold Sparrow, Assistant Superintendent Muriel Leonard, Superintendent Steve Leonard, Bishop Gilbert Thompson, and the Honorable Mayor Thomas Menino.

Thanks to our interns and research assistants Heather Ross, Emily Wood, Jana Pinto, Emily Graef, and Tia Fowler, and to all those we may have forgotten to mention but who are dear to our hearts.

We hope that we will continue to work together until every child in America realizes it's cool to be smart, and reaches their full potential in school and in life.

Table of Contents

Introduction   1

Why We Are Qualified to Write This Guidebook   5

The Inspiration for The BIFF Paradigm Project   7

Motivation Makes the Difference   13

10 Tips to Motivate Your Child to Get A's in School   17

1. Touch and Tell   19

2. Switch Airwaves to Brainwaves   23

3. Become a High School Drop-In   27

4. Help Teachers the United Way   33

5. Use Peer Pressure as Kryptonite   37

6. Set Up a Visualizing Wall   41

7. Don't Guess, Test!   45

8. Raise Your Trouble Threshold   49

9. Identify Your Child's Learning Style   53

10. Pay Your Child for A's   57

101 Inspirational Quotes for Struggling Students   71

About the Authors   79

BIFF Millionaire Mindboost 2-Day Motivation and Study   81
Skills Seminar

APPENDIX   85

A Special Report: What Your Teen Doesn't Want You to   87
Know About the Student Motivation Crisis in American
Schools

Student Motivation Survey for Parents   93

Student Motivation Survey Self-Assessment (for Students)   97

Tell a Friend About Stop Flunking!   101

Motivation Minute Newsletter   103

Bibliography   105

Contact Us   107

The problem is
that your child is not
motivated...

Introduction

"I am so sick of the grades my child keeps bringing home, I don't know what to do. What on earth does he think he's going to do with his life with grades like this? If you don't know how to do something, that's one thing, but when you know what to do and you're just too lazy to do it, or you just don't care to do it? ... I give up! I've tried everything. I talked, I screamed, I yelled, I took away his video games, the TV, his music. I'd even take away his bed if I thought it would work. Please help me!"

We have listened to a thousand variations of this story for the past ten years, and my wife and I know your pain. I'm Gary Bracey, and my wife is Ayele Shakur, and we have spent the last decade fixing this problem and we don't use ancient Chinese torture.

Okay, so you've got a teenager or a pre-teen in school, and he or she (I'll switch at will) is driving you nuts. He's bright, he's charismatic, he could be getting A's and B's if he wanted to, but he just doesn't seem to care. You've probably tried everything. You've lectured, fussed, put him on punishment, and probably visited his teachers at school. Nothing really seems to work. And when you occasionally find something that does, the results don't last that long.

The problem is that your child is not motivated—at least not when it comes to school. She's probably motivated to watch TV, or go shopping, or listen to music—and she's certainly motivated when it comes to hanging out with friends. Yet when it comes to buckling down and doing homework, getting to school on time, and paying attention in class, motivation flies right out the window.

Low academic
motivation is a
silent epidemic that's
sweeping its way across
America.

Don't blame yourself. The fact is, low academic motivation is a silent epidemic that's sweeping its way across America, from the inner cities to the suburbs. For most students, the low motivation bug creeps in shortly after the 4th grade and hangs around like a bad case of acne right through high school.

You can learn more about this
low-motivation epidemic
by reading our Special Report in the Appendix:

What Your Teen Doesn't Want You to Know
About the Student Motivation Crisis
in American Schools

Back in 1998, my wife and I created a unique motivational program called BIFF (Building Inspiration From Failure). BIFF transforms failing teens into Honor Roll students. Most of the kids who come to our program have C's, D's, and F's, and don't really care. For them, attending summer school is like heading off to camp—it happens almost every year. In the worst cases, some of these kids are chronically late for school, cutting classes, or repeatedly absent. And sadly, some of them are in danger of dropping out of school altogether. We have successfully used our motivational methods to help turn their lives around.

If you're a parent who wants to see your child shift towards a more positive attitude ... if you need her to put more effort into schoolwork and homework ... if you want your mediocre or failing child to become excellent at "the game of school," then this guidebook is for you.

Can we fix your
challenging problem?
The answer is yes.

Why We Are Qualified to Write This Guidebook

I'm going to go over this part fairly quickly, because you probably don't care what degrees we have or schools we've attended. You're not interested in the fact that my wife has a master's degree from Harvard's Graduate School of Education or that she was a public school teacher for 11 years. You probably don't care that we run a nonprofit tutoring center in Boston that's been in existence for over 25 years, or that for the past eight years we've specialized in helping over 1,000 failing, unmotivated teenagers to excel in school. You might not even care to know that we tested and tweaked our motivational strategies on our own teenage son, who was the epitome of "bright but lazy" but who graduated from Boston College High School with A's and B's while holding down a full-time job at Toys "R" Us®. Now that's motivation!

You're not interested in our history or qualifications, or the experience we bring to our profession. All you care about is can we fix your challenging problem now? The answer is yes. The biggest reason is because I was an unmotivated child myself. In fact, it was because I gave my parents such a hard time growing up that I was able to help create one of the most successful programs for student motivation in the country—The BIFF Paradigm Project—and I'm now able to share some of the important secrets of BIFF's success. Here's my story.

My father was
Dr. Martin Luther
King Jr.'s bodyguard.

The Inspiration for
The BIFF Paradigm Project:
A Motivational Learning-Skills
Program

My father was Dr. Martin Luther King Jr.'s bodyguard. Many people don't know or have forgotten that back in 1958, Dr. King was stabbed by a paranoid schizophrenic bag lady while at a book signing in Harlem. When they took Dr. King to Harlem Hospital, the investigating police asked him if he personally knew anyone on the police force that he would like to have protect him whenever he was in town. "Yes, Sergeant Bracey," Dr. King said, "President of The Guardians." The Guardians Association is an organization of Black police officers in New York City that my father helped create some years earlier. It seemed only fitting that the President of the Guardians would be hand-picked to head security for Dr. King. So whenever Dr. King or anyone in his family came to New York, my father, Sergeant Bracey of the NYPD, would accompany them around the Big Apple.

I remember one night in the winter of 1963 when Mrs. King, Dr. Martin Luther King Jr.'s mother, came by our house in Queens for a visit. We lived just a short cab ride from Idlewild Airport, known today as JFK Airport, and the Kings would come straight to our house and wait for my father. On this particular night, my father wasn't home. He had gone to Open School to get my report card. My teachers usually described me as a "bright but mischievous boy," and in the 6th grade, I was failing almost everything. I figured there was no point in doing much work before spring. That's when you really had to buckle down

I was one of those kids
who could claim the
principal's office as a
permanent living address.

so you didn't have to go to summer school. I figured that, aside from staying out of summer school, what was the point of doing any school-work? No one could ever accuse me of being a cop's goody-two-shoes son. I was one of those kids who could claim the principal's office as a permanent living address.

When Mrs. King arrived that night in 1963, I encouraged her to wait for my father to get home. I fluffed up pillows on the couch before she sat down, poured her a glass of ice-cold lemonade, and offered her a sandwich. She sat with church-lady charm, her hands folded on her lap with a gentle smile on her lips while I rambled on with stories about our visit to see relatives in Barbados, where my mother's family was from. I hated our trip to Barbados—it was hot and sticky with plenty of big flies and no air conditioning—but I was determined to keep Mrs. King from leaving. I figured no matter how bad the teachers' reports were, Dad wouldn't kill me if Mrs. King were there as a witness.

Sure enough, when my father came home, the temperature in the room rose fifty degrees. He held my report card tightly in his hand, and his thick eyebrows furrowed over his deep gray eyes. I said a quick good night to Mrs. King and scurried upstairs to give Dad a chance to cool off, but I didn't go right to my room. Instead, I stopped at the top of the stairs where I could overhear their conversation below.

The living-room chair groaned when my father sat down and began his mile-long laundry list of problems my teachers told him about me. My father, a very powerful man, was used to having things done his way. He would eventually rise through the ranks to become the first Black chief over all five boroughs of the NYC police department. But tonight he was a completely frustrated father when it came to my bad conduct and sorry grades. When he was done telling Mrs. King his woes, he raked his fingers over his shiny bald head in exasperation.

"Mrs. King," he said with a sigh, "how did you get M.L. to get good grades when he was in school?"

"Mrs. King," he said with a sigh, "how did you get M.L. (what family and friends called Martin Luther King Jr.) to get good grades when he was in school?"

"Oh, well, that was easy," Mrs. King said with quiet confidence, as if she were teaching Sunday school. "If he brought home an A, I'd give him a quarter. If he brought home a B, I'd give him a dime. He liked the money, so he always brought home good grades."

I was at the top of the stairs wearing a huge grin and rubbing my hands together, thinking of the piles of money I would make. Mrs. King was a preacher's wife and Martin Luther King Jr.'s mother—what better authority could you want? This was money in the bank. What she said was gospel. So I thought. Unfortunately, my father was not ready to receive her pious wisdom. He never gave me a dime. To this day, I'll never understand why not. If he had paid me, I definitely would have brought home good grades.

He had no problem paying me to shine his shoes. Why? Was he trying to make me a shoeshine boy? He had no problem paying me to wash his car. Why? Was he training me to work at a carwash? He paid me to take out the trash. Was he trying to make me a sanitation engineer? Like most parents, he told me over and over again that school was my job, but he never paid me anything to do the most important job of my young life. He never took Mrs. King's advice.

Forty years later, I took Mrs. King's advice and used it as a central component in BIFF (Building Inspiration From Failure), which turns failing teenagers into highly successful students. I will give you a detailed explanation of how to implement Mrs. King's idea for using cash incentives to get your child to bring home A's every day. But first let's take a closer look at motivation as the most important ingredient for helping your child do well in school, and in life.

Motivation is the key
ingredient that makes the
difference between
F's and A's.

Motivation Makes the Difference

My wife and I have worked with over a thousand teens in Boston since BIFF began. We start out with the toughest kids, the ones that most people have given up on—the D and F students, the ones we affectionately refer to as "the bottom-dwellers." Within a year, seventy eight percent of our BIFF Alumni are passing all of their classes with a C average or higher.

Twenty-five percent make dramatic turnarounds, going from failing to the Honor Roll with A's and B's. Eighty-five percent report an improved attitude about school and life. Through BIFF, our kids have gone from failure to excellence in under a year.

Getting a student to do well in school, to complete homework assignments, to participate in class, to score high on tests, to concentrate, to focus, to learn, all begins with one small seed—motivation. Motivation is the key ingredient that makes the difference between F's and A's. Motivation makes the difference between failure and success.

The following 10 Tips have been tried and tested over the past eight years that we have been doing the BIFF Program. They have helped hundreds of failing and mediocre students to become highly motivated and successful in school. We're sure they will do the same for your child.

STOP!

Before you continue reading this book, you should first take our Student Motivation Survey for Parents. This survey is designed to help parents pinpoint their child's motivational needs. To take the survey, go to <u>www.student-motivation-for-better-grades.com</u> and click where it says: "Click here to take our Free student motivation survey to identify your child's motivation quotient."

"Nearly half a century ago, educational philosopher John Dewey and others claimed that if schools were to succeed in preparing the great majority of young people, not just a select few, to be responsible and productive citizens, they would have to do a much better job of motivating and engaging the broad spectrum of students in learning."
-from *Engaging Schools*

For best results, the survey should be completed by both the parent and the child. In this way, the survey can become a learning tool that helps to stimulate discussion about the child's motivational level and school performance. After taking the survey, you will get **INSTANT RESULTS** along with instructions on how to interpret your score.

If you do not have internet access, please refer to the Appendix where you will find both the Student Motivation Survey for Parents and the Student Motivation Survey Self-Assessment (For Students). There is also a Student Motivation Survey for Guidance Counselors, Teachers, and School Administrators, available online, which you might want to share with your child's school.

"People often say that motivation doesn't last. Well, neither does bathing - that's why we recommend it daily."
-Zig Ziglar

10 TIPS TO MOTIVATE YOUR CHILD TO GET A'S IN SCHOOL

1. Touch and Tell
2. Switch Airwaves to Brainwaves
3. Become a High School Drop-In
4. Help Teachers the United Way
5. Use Peer Pressure as Kryptonite
6. Set Up a Visualizing Wall
7. Don't Guess, Test
8. Raise Your Trouble Threshold
9. Identify Your Child's Learning Style
10. Pay Your Child for A's

BIFF PRINCIPLE:

Make small
accomplishments
a BIG DEAL.

1. Touch and Tell

We had a student that went through our 6-week BIFF program whose report card grade in algebra went from an F during the first marking term to an A- by the end of the second marking term. History had gone from an F to a C, and English had gone from a D- to a B-. He brought his report card to the Boston Learning Center to show it to my wife and I.

"What changed, Larry?" Ayele asked, as she stood in front of the photocopier to memorialize the report card. "How did you manage to get such incredible grades?"

"I figured I'd try and use some of that stuff you guys taught us in BIFF," he said. He wore a brilliant smile.

"Well it's about time," Ayele said, smiling back.

He shrugged. "Yeah, I guess so."

"I'm proud of you, Larry. You should be really proud of yourself." Ayele handed his report card back to him.

"Yeah, but I'm not gonna bother to do it again," he said, folding up his report card and shoving it into his back pocket. "I showed my dad, and he didn't even care."

Are some parents too preoccupied with the chaos in their own lives to pay any attention when their child brings home a great report card? Unfortunately, yes.

Whenever your child brings home an A or B paper, recognize the accomplishment. We've had many kids in BIFF come to us and say, "I brought home an A paper but my parents didn't even notice." We know you're busy, but take time to notice the things your teen is doing right instead of the things he's doing wrong. Even though your child may not

BIFF PRINCIPLE:

Take time when they do things right to talk them through their thinking process.

be doing well in school right now, it's very important that your child knows you disapprove of his grades, not that you disapprove of him. Make small accomplishments a BIG DEAL.

Before I became an educator, I ran one of the largest minority-owned printing companies in New England. I have been an employer of people most of my life, as was my father before me. When one of my employees does something wrong or makes a mistake, I do not spend a lot of time on the error. I don't waste time on explanations or reasons for what went wrong. Instead, I take time when they do things *right* to talk them through their thinking process, and in that way reinforce correct thinking and the positive outcomes it produces. I have found in business that some people are starving for attention—any attention, even if it's negative.

Make sure your child gets the positive attention he needs for the good and right things he does. And don't forget the power of touch. It doesn't matter how old your child is. Even teenagers need a pat on the back or a warm hug to help reinforce your approval and praise. As Dr. James Comer points out in *Leave No Child Behind: Preparing Today's Youth for Tomorrow's World*, "Children who receive more praise in their families achieve at a higher academic level than others."

During our consultation sessions, we have encountered many parents who will talk to us with a pleasant look on their face, but whenever they turn to look at their child they wear a snarl. That has to have a negative effect on the child. Home should never be a battleground. No matter how bad things are going at school, smile and let your child know you love her. A big hug, a little smile, some positive conversations about what went right will go a long way. Try it. We know it might not be easy at first, but this really works. And the more you do it, the easier it gets.

BIFF PRINCIPLE:

Be doers
and not watchers
of the doers.

2. Switch Airwaves to Brainwaves

Okay, this one's for you as well as for your child. Research proves that the more TV your child watches, the worse he will perform in school. It's that simple. There's a reason they call it the boob tube. If you want your child to watch less TV, you'll have to lead by example. Turn off that TV and take out a daily newspaper, a magazine, or a good book instead. Kids need to see that reading is not punishment or something that just happens at school.

What did people do before TV was invented? About 10 years ago, my lovely wife came up with the brilliant idea that we should remove the TV from the bedroom. I have to admit I was a little slow to embrace the idea. I was used to sleeping with the TV on. It was the first thing I saw in the morning and the last thing at night. Try that for a while and tell me you're smarter.

None of the good things that have happened to us over the years would have been possible without that small step of removing the TV from the bedroom. I know we would have never created BIFF or written this book, and sometimes I wonder if we might not even still be together. Getting rid of the TV has created so much more quality time. I know that it is hard to turn your back on instant entertainment, but we need to be doers and not watchers of the doers.

I was on a beach in the Bahamas at sunrise a couple of winters ago with my brother-in-law Charles. This early morning ritual of watching the sunrise was something we had both developed alone, apart from each other. But on this particular morning we found ourselves outside together, twenty minutes after sunrise, and deep in conversation as if it were midday and not an hour past daybreak.

BIFF PRINCIPLE:

Kids who watch 3 hours or more of TV each day have the highest chance of dropping out of school.

Charles said to me that morning, "The only difference between me and Donald Trump is what we do with our 24 hours." Although there were quite a few differences between Charles and "The Donald," I listened to his explanation. "I know, for example, that he's not watching television or playing video games," he said. "God gives us all 24 hours a day, and it's up to us how we use them."

According to a recent Kaiser Family Foundation study, children ages 8 to 18 watch about three hours of television per day. Time spent in front of a television set is time *not* spent studying and doing homework. Of course, some kids try to study *in front of* the TV set—and the results are never surprising.

Researchers have linked TV time to academic achievement and even graduation rates. For example, one Stanford University and Johns Hopkins University study found that children with televisions in their bedrooms scored significantly lower on standardized tests than children who watched the same amount of TV, but do not have bedroom sets. Another study found that kids who watch 3 hours or more of TV each day have the highest chance of dropping out of school.

The American Academy of Pediatrics recommends that kids watch no more than 2 hours of TV per day and that children under 2 years old watch none at all. How much television do your kids watch, and how much television do your kids see *you* watch? Try turning the TV off for a week, and see how much more your entire family is able to accomplish.

BIFF PRINCIPLE:

Parental involvement
increases academic
performance.

3. Become a High School Drop-In

We know you're busy, but when there's an event taking place at your child's school, you have to show up. One of the greatest factors that affect a student's motivation to excel in school is parental involvement. Many parents are highly involved in their child's education during the elementary years, but research shows that as children progress though middle and high school, parental involvement drops off sharply.

Ironically, it's during the adolescent years, when teens naturally become less attached to their parents, that parental involvement becomes vitally important. Parental involvement increases academic performance. It has a positive effect on dropout rates, and it reduces teen involvement in destructive behaviors such as drug use and sex.

There are many different forms of parental involvement. You might volunteer to help out in the classroom, or serve on the parent council. You might help your child at home with homework and give your child encouragement and advice when she needs it. You probably already do a lot with your child at home behind the scenes, but one of the greatest forms of parental involvement is getting out of your home and actually showing up at school.

As a 6th grade social studies teacher, when my wife's middle school would hold an Open House, even though she had about 104 students she worked with each day, usually about twelve parents would show up. Of those twelve parents, about ten of them had kids who were already A and B students. The parents of her D and F students rarely came.

BIFF PRINCIPLE:

Many parents just don't understand how important it is to show up at school.

Did the A and B students get that way because their parents came to school events, or did their parents come because they had A and B students and wanted to hear good reports? I don't think it's because the D and F parents didn't care. Parents love their children and want what's best for them. Many parents just don't understand how important it is to show up at school.

One year, we held a parent breakfast in September to introduce the BIFF program to parents at the school. The brunch was complete with scrambled eggs, grits, home fries, fried chicken, beans and rice, jerk chicken, bacon, and sausage. Our older BIFF kids provided babysitting in one of the classrooms, which was turned into a mini movie theatre. The event was free, and parents were welcome to bring as many of their hungry children as they wanted.

I was expecting at least 150 people to come out to our breakfast. After all, I was a businessman, not an educator. The school had over 600 students enrolled, so 150 people including students and parents would equate to only about twenty percent, which seemed to me a reasonable turnout. By the end of the morning, we only had forty-eight parents and a ton of leftover food. I was devastated. It was my first exposure to the world of low parental involvement.

I had passed out flyers, made phone calls, and done everything I knew to get a good turnout. While I was standing in a corner moping, the school principal came over to congratulate me on such a wonderful event. She was impressed with the turnout, and said it was the most parents she had ever seen at a school event that wasn't connected to sports or a play.

Still not convinced that you should show up more often at your child's school? You probably have lots of good excuses for not showing up. But let's face it. If you had to catch a plane to the Bahamas,

BIFF PRINCIPLE:

Show up *unexpectedly* during the school day.

you'd be there, wouldn't you? If you knew you were going to receive a big lottery check, you'd be there wouldn't you? It's all about establishing priorities. If you really want your child to think school is important, then make sure you ALWAYS show up.

When you show up at school, if you have moved recently or changed phone numbers, make sure that your child's teachers and the secretary in the main office all have your correct contact information. This may seem obvious, but you'd be surprised. Many kids today have managed to outsmart their parents. They have figured out, and spread the word to each other, that if the school cannot contact you because they don't have your correct phone number, then the child is free to do whatever she wants to in school. It happens more often than you might think. So if nothing else, you need to make sure the school has correct contact information for you. And when teachers have your phone number handy, they'll be more apt to contact you as soon as they see any early warning signs of trouble with your child's school performance.

If you really want to make a big splash, show up *unexpectedly* during the school day and drop in on a few of your child's classes. When your child sees you in the hallways at school, or sitting in a seat behind him a few rows back, it will send a powerful message that you care about his education. If your child is like most teens, he'll be so mortified and embarrassed that he'll start bringing home A's just to make sure that never happens again!

BIFF PRINCIPLE:

The teacher
is always
right.

4. Help Teachers the United Way

You have to work with your child's teachers, not against them. Okay, you might have a teacher who's a real jerk, or maybe more than one. But trashing a teacher in front of your child will only empower your child to make excuses and not do the teacher's work. That's the wrong message and will only make matters worse.

If you express disrespect toward the teacher, you're giving your child license to do the same. The teacher is ultimately in charge of the situation. The teacher's the one deciding the grades at the end of the term. The difference between a B- and a C+ is just one small percentage point. What good can it do to make the teacher an enemy?

When my wife and I were kids, our parents taught us that the teacher was always right. If a conflict arose with the teacher, according to our parents we were automatically wrong and the teacher's word was sacred. Now, our parents might have secretly taken issue with something a teacher said or did, but they would schedule a parent-teacher conference and meet PRIVATELY to discuss that issue. The teacher was never confronted within earshot or eyeshot where we could see or hear what went on. And when our parents returned home, the teacher was somehow still always right. The teacher was part of the team and there was never any dissention among the ranks of the team. This is a very important rule that you should always follow (even if you secretly work behind the scenes to change your child's teacher.) Never give your child a sense of power over an adult in authority or you will live to regret it.

Too many parents today have created an atmosphere of disrespect for the teacher, which is often played out in front of the student. If you believe that teachers are there to be challenged, teachers are wrong, and

BIFF PRINCIPLE:

If you must confront a teacher, always do it in private.

teachers are out to get your child, then your child will believe this too. So never make a negative comment about the teacher or pit yourself against the teacher in front of your child. If you must confront a teacher, always do it in private. Always praise the teachers in front of your child and point out the good things they are doing. Let your child know you are 100% behind their teachers.

In private, you can still give them hell. But always remember that you are not going to be in that classroom every day—your child will. I'm reminded of a time when my father was living in a nursing home. In the latter stages of Alzheimer's disease and having suffered a stroke, this once powerful man was completely dependent on others for his care. On occasion and for one reason or another, I had problems with the performance of an attendant. When confronting the attendant, I always had to keep in mind that I was not going to be there 24/7. My methods in handling the problems my dad faced had to be effective when I was there, and even more so when I was not.

True wisdom in dealing with a problem shouldn't inflame or polarize the parties involved, but instead unite and bring harmony to the situation. If you need to confront your child's teacher about an issue, remember your child, just like my father, still has to function in the environment you helped to create.

BIFF PRINCIPLE:

Studying with a buddy
is smart.
Studying in a group is
even smarter.

5. Use Peer Pressure as Kryptonite

Peer pressure is one of the most powerful forces in a teenager's world. It is pure kryptonite when used correctly. We use it to our advantage when teaching in front of a classroom of unmotivated teenagers, and you can use it to your advantage as a parent.

One of the best ways to create positive peer pressure is by helping your child form a study group. Studying with a buddy is smart. Studying in a group is even smarter. Kids can cover more material in less time if they divide and share the work. Let's face it—kids want to socialize, so why not encourage them to socialize around schoolwork? Better yet, why not encourage them to socialize in your home, where you can meet their friends and classmates? Wouldn't it be great if you could put a face and even a personality to the names you always hear?

Have your child invite his friends over, set up some healthy snacks, and let them work at the kitchen table. (Watch the sugar, or you will never do it again.) You can also encourage your child to coordinate a study space at the local library if your home won't do. Our exit surveys show that most of our kids think learning to study together is one of the most helpful strategies they learn in BIFF. As one alumnus put it, "I like working and learning together and feeling like I'm part of a team."

On the other hand, negative peer pressure often motivates bright students to underachieve or even to fail, particularly at the middle and high-school level where image is everything. During the turbulent teen years, the negative influence of a student's peer group is stronger than your parental disapproval, getting grounded, earning low grades, or even being disciplined at school. That's why it's so important for you to foster positive peer pressure. We are always telling our children who

BIFF PRINCIPLE:

Try saying, "What great question did you ask in school today?"

we *don't* want them to hang out with and what we *don't* want them to do. We need to let them know what we like them to do and which of their friends we like and why. We can do this best by creating a positive friendly environment like a study group.

Other ways you can create a positive peer environment is to put up a basketball hoop, cook Saturday or Sunday breakfast for the kids, or even coach a team. When you have them all together, ask them thought-provoking questions that need more than a one-word answer. For example, parents often ask, "How was school today?" and get that bland one-word answer, "Fine..."

Instead, try saying "What great question did you ask in school today?" When you get that blank stare from the kids, say, "Okay, what *good* question did you ask?" Then poll the responses to, "Was that a good question?" Soon they will be competing for who asked the best questions, especially if you give something extra to the agreed-upon winner.

Creating positive peer pressure is one of the best things you can do as a parent. One study of at-risk students found that "seventy-seven percent of those who reported that all or most of their friends placed high importance on learning went on to enroll in a four-year college, compared to fifty-five percent of those whose friends placed less importance on education and learning." [i] Other research suggests that students with high-achieving friends are less likely to drop out of school. When friends are all moving in the right direction, that's exactly what friends are for.

BIFF PRINCIPLE:

"Whatever the mind of man can conceive and believe it can achieve."
-Napoleon Hill

6. Set Up a Visualizing Wall

How did our son get A's and B's in high school while working 40 hours a week at Toys "R" Us®? He had a goal. He wanted to buy a motorcycle as a graduation present at the end of his senior year. As parents, we didn't like this goal. The idea of our son the speed demon, popping wheelies while racing down city streets on a Ninja®, was far from consoling. But we couldn't deny how powerful that goal was as a motivator for him.

On the wall above the desk where he studied each night, our son had cut-out magazine pictures of the motorcycle he was planning to one day own. It was his visualizing wall. Since we were using the cash-incentives plan inspired by Dr. Martin Luther King Jr.'s mother, our son knew his good grades would pay off. Our unmotivated son became highly motivated almost overnight.

In BIFF, one of our first lessons is to have each kid cut out a picture from a magazine of something they would like to someday own as a result of their hard work. We have them tape this picture on the wall right above where they do most of their studying. It's a simple form of motivation that works!

Psychologist Maxwell Marx once said, "The mind cannot tell the difference between what is real and what is vividly imagined." Author Napoleon Hill who wrote *Think and Grow Rich* said, "Whatever the mind of man can conceive and believe it can achieve." Both men were right.

So how do you get a failing student who has never been on the Honor Roll to believe that it's possible? Here's how: Get his subconscious mind to vividly imagine that it has already happened, and that

BIFF PRINCIPLE:

If you want your child to
become an A student,
you have to first
help her believe that
she *is* an A student.

the results are even better than expected. His mind will move his actions toward that visualized goal. (More about this process in a later book.)

If you want your child to become an A student, you have to first help her believe that she *is* an A student. In BIFF, we use a technique called Positive Visualization to help students "see and believe" that they are successful. It doesn't take long before success becomes part of their reality.

Since Positive Visualization is too detailed to include as part of this guidebook, we recommend that you use self-hypnosis CDs with your child. Self-hypnosis is a safe, fun, and relaxing way to reprogram the subconscious mind to believe and achieve.

Visit the website www.hypnosis-audio.com for a fabulous selection of audio CDs on topics like *Paying Attention in School, Homework Hurdles, Educational Excellence, Test Relaxing,* and *Performance Anxiety.* They have many great topics for adults too. You'll be amazed at how these audio CDs help to "reprogram" your child as a successful learner. And because they are so relaxing, they are a wonderful sleep aid for teenagers who never seem to get enough rest.

BIFF PRINCIPLE:

Make sure it's really a motivational issue and not a skills-based one.

7. Don't Guess, Test!

Is your child getting poor grades in school because he's unmotivated, or is there something bigger going on? The fact is, if your child is having skills-based problems, then no amount of motivation is going to help him bring home A's. By all means, you need to make sure it's really a motivational issue and not a skills-based one. If you're not sure, have your child tested.

If you're worried about having your child labeled as "special needs," then seek an independent evaluation at a tutoring center or at one of the children's hospitals in your area. Many tutoring centers and children's hospitals offer what's called a CORE Evaluation to determine if a child has any learning disabilities. A CORE Evaluation is a comprehensive series of tests designed to determine if your child is in need of special education services. The CORE evaluation may include any of the following:

- Psycho-educational assessment
- Home assessment
- Health assessment
- Educational assessment
- Student observation

These tests and evaluations can range anywhere from $75 – $1,000 or more, depending on how extensive the testing. But it's worth it to have the peace of mind of knowing if a learning disability is the true cause behind your child's F's.

BIFF PRINCIPLE:

Don't ignore signs that
your child needs help if
you spot them.

Since my wife and I run a nonprofit tutoring center in Boston, we often meet parents who are in denial and refuse to have their child tested. (We charge $75 - $150 for an educational assessment.) Don't ignore signs that your child needs help if you spot them. A child who is legitimately struggling in school because of a learning disability will often disengage or become disruptive in school, and might ultimately drop out. Early detection is the key. The sooner you find out if your child has a learning disability, the sooner you can get help. There are effective solutions and methods to overcome most learning challenges. In some cases, the solution is as simple as getting prescription eyeglasses or having your child's seat moved from the back to the front of the classroom.

Whether your child has a documented learning disability, or if she just needs help in a specific area, there are places like our Boston Learning Center (www.bostonlearningcenter.org) where she can get tutoring. If your child attends an underperforming school, you might be able to get this tutoring free of charge through the federal No Child Left Behind Act. Ask your school principal for details.

In our everyday lives, people develop habits. Winning is a habit just as losing is a habit. Help develop your child's winning ways by getting the help they need early.

You can learn more about FREE Tutoring by reading our Special Report: *How to Get Free Tutoring for Your Child Through No Child Left Behind.* **Visit:**
www.student-motivation-for-better-grades.com/nochildleftbehind.html

---

BIFF PRINCIPLE:

Parents can have low expectations for their own children.

8. Raise Your Trouble Threshold

A parent came to the Boston Learning Center to enroll her child in BIFF and tutoring. She sat in our initial consultation interview bemoaning the fact that her child was lazy, was not doing any work, and would rather watch TV than study. This poor mother was spending these trying teenage years locked in constant battles with her son. After she had laid out a laundry list of everything wrong with her child, she slumped back in her chair, lifted her eyes up to the ceiling as if she were calling on a higher power, and with a deep sigh, she said, "If only he could bring home a 'C' I'd be happy."

I leapt to my feet, ran to the door, checked the hall to make sure no one heard her (for special effect), and ran back to her saying, "Never, ever let anyone hear you say that again. Especially your child."

So much literature is written about teachers having low expectations for their students, but often, parents can have low expectations for their own children. Okay, so of course you don't want your child to fail. But have you given up hope that your child can excel? Are you sending your child a message that average is good enough?

What is the "trouble threshold" in your household? In his book *Beyond the Classroom: Why School Reform has Failed and What Parents Need to Do*, author Laurence Steinberg defines the "trouble threshold" as the lowest grade your child can bring home before he knows he will be in trouble. In his research, Steinberg found that interesting differences existed in the trouble threshold based on the culture of the household.

BIFF PRINCIPLE:

"If anyone ever calls you average, you should get insulted."

Not surprisingly, the trouble threshold was highest in Asian families, where anything less than an A- was cause for alarm. In White households, it was a full grade lower, with anything less than a B- being an issue. In Black and Latino households, students only got in trouble when they brought home something lower than a C-. Higher expectations explain why Asian students generally do better in school than any other ethnic group.

Parental expectations, and for students, the fear of getting their parents upset, make all the difference. Tell your child what you expect, and your child will try to give it to you. My father used to tell me, and I repeat this message in BIFF, "If anyone ever calls you average, you should get insulted, because the average person isn't very bright." In BIFF, our scholars know we do not like C's, and the only reason we like B's is because a B is the next-closest thing to an A. An "A" means you have fully mastered the material.

Understand this—a C is average. If you are pushing your child to "at least bring home C's" and he misses the mark, he will end up with D's and F's. But if you are pushing your child to be excellent and get A's, then even if he misses the mark, he will still end up above average with B's.

Always push your child to get A's. And make sure that anything less than a B is cause for concern. Always have high expectations for your child. And whenever those high expectations are met, remember to give a smile, a hug, and a reward. (In the long run, the rewards won't be needed as much. But for now, while you're trying to turn your child's grades around, never forget the rewards.) For an extra reinforcement, ask your child for a detailed explanation of how they achieved this excellent grade, so they can *speak* as well as *hear* the process they used to achieve excellence.

BIFF PRINCIPLE:

It cuts your learning time
in half when you
understand how you
learn best.

9. Identify Your Child's Learning Style

The basis in learning is to understand *how* you learn, and that each person learns differently. In BIFF, we focus on three basic learning styles: visual, auditory, and kinesthetic. As the names imply, the visual learner learns best by what he can see, such as the blackboard, a book, or a picture. The auditory learner learns by hearing things, such as the teacher's voice, a tape, a rhyme, or music. The kinesthetic learner learns by what he can touch and do, such as participating in a project or a play, or working with a mentor. Even adults need to understand their learning styles, because it cuts your learning time in half when you understand how you learn best.

We have found that about sixty-eight-percent of our unmotivated students in BIFF are auditory and kinesthetic learners. Most classroom teaching is done toward a visual learner, so it is not surprising that our students are having a hard time in school. The way they learn and the way their teachers teach is totally disconnected. It's not that students cannot learn in learning styles that are not their own. They can. Just like a person born in China can learn in English, of course they can. But first, they have to convert the lesson to their language. This conversion itself can be a tremendous learning tool. It's best for them to harness the power of their own learning styles, and to convert what they are being taught into a language that their brains readily accept. No matter what one's learning style, the conversion process is a good thing for long-term memory.

For example, if your child is trying to master vocabulary words and she is a visual learner, flashcards would be helpful. If your child is an auditory learner, she should use a tape recorder to record the words and

BIFF PRINCIPLE:

The more learning modes you use to learn something new, the better you will know the subject.

definitions, and then play back the recording on her Walkman®. If your child is a kinesthetic learner, he should get up and act out each word and its definition, or perhaps create word puzzles to help memorize the words. We tell kids, "If you really want to be sure that you know something, learn it in all three styles." The more learning modes you use to learn something new, the better you will know the subject.

As the youngest of three children in the family, I used to memorize television commercials fastest when we were growing up. My brother, sister, and I would play a game to see who could say the commercials word-for-word the fastest. Who could learn the jingle first? I often came in first, and at the time, would have thought myself to be an auditory learner. But after being tested, I now know I am a kinesthetic learner, and realize I would act the commercials out and remember the words and gestures. I put all three learning styles together and memorized faster than my older siblings.

The best way to identify your child's learning style, as well as your own, is to go to www.howtolearn.com and take their free Learning Styles Assessment. Tell them BIFF sent you.

BIFF PRINCIPLE:

Hard work in school
pays off.

10. Pay Your Child for A's

We know this is a controversial suggestion, but it works for many unmotivated students. In fact, when we survey parents at the end of the BIFF Program and ask them what BIFF strategies, if any, they are using at home, the overwhelming majority say they are using cash incentives.

Parents will often say, "Well, I don't know about giving my child money for grades. She should do it just for education's sake. She should want to get as much out of school as she can anyway." To this we always ask, "Did you?" That always seems to stop them in their tracks.

Most parents who come to the Boston Learning Center have to admit that they weren't great students themselves, and they almost without exception decide that using cash incentives isn't such a bad idea. After all, nothing else so far has worked.

We live in a capitalistic society. Everything of value has a price tag on it. If we say education is the most valuable thing a child should be doing with their time, why don't we put some substance to these words? Don't we mean what we are saying? Shouldn't we help kids see in some concrete way that hard work in school pays off? Mrs. King believed in this method for young Martin, and my wife and I have used it to great success in our own family and in the BIFF Program.

Occasionally when I talk to the parent of a failing student about using cash incentives, the parent will say, "Oh, I already tried that." The child is usually staring back at his parent in utter disbelief. This is the point where I will ask the child to leave the room.

BIFF PRINCIPLE:

For incentives to be effective, the child must believe that the reward is actually available and attainable.

Once the child is gone, I explain to the parent that cash incentives are probably not working because the child does not believe the parent will actually deliver on the promise. Although we as parents can never remember a time—except that one time—when we broke a promise to our children, our children have volumes of books and records of what they consider broken promises made by their parents. For incentives to be effective, the child must believe that the reward is actually available and attainable. After I discuss the details of the BIFF Incentives Plan and how it should work, I bring the child back into the room.

"Do you have any tests coming up this week?" I ask.

"I have a science test this Friday," the child answers, usually looking quite skeptical and not exactly sure where this is going.

"What are you going to get on the test?"

He says, not very convincingly, "I'm pretty sure I'm going to pass."

"Well, what will it take for you to get an A?" I ask.

"I don't know."

"Well, if I give you a dollar will you get an A?" The child usually says yes, although some kids hold out for five. I take the bill and rip it in half, to the shock and amazement of both the parent and child. Then I hand half to the child and say, "This is your money. This other half won't do me any good, and all you need to do to get this half from me is bring me that A paper." Believing is no longer a problem.

BIFF PRINCIPLE:

"For where your
treasure is,
there your heart
will be also."
-Matthew 6:21, NIV

After this demonstration, some parents enroll their child in BIFF, and some do not. Many parents who choose not to enroll have come back to us later and said, "I no longer need your program. My child is bringing home A's all the time now."

Kids aren't to blame if they don't care about school when they're living in what pop singer Madonna called a "material world." After all, they live in a society that targets them as one of the fastest-growing consumer markets on the planet. The teen market is a $124-billion industry, so kids today are bombarded with hundreds of commercials on their televisions, radios, and even pop-ups on the Internet. Buy this, buy that. They are not treated as kids, but as consumers. So in our materialistic world, anything that does not have a price tag attached must not have any value. There is a passage in the Bible that says, "For where your treasure is, there your heart will be also" (Matthew 6:21, NIV). And often in our lives, our "treasure" is represented by money and material possessions. Connect money to grades, and see where your child's heart lies.

Here's how the BIFF Incentives Plan works. Each and every time your child comes home from school with an "A" paper on any size homework assignment, test, or quiz (no matter how small), pay them at least one quarter. Do it right on the spot. Don't put it off until later. Show your child that "A" is important by paying him for a job well done.

Over the years we have found that just one little quarter goes a long way with kids of all ages—yes, even teenagers! It's the symbol that counts, more than the monetary value. Some parents pay a little more for a test or quiz than they do for a regular homework assignment, but it's entirely up to you.

BIFF PRINCIPLE:

You can change the increments in the incentive plan to as much or as little as you like… Just be consistent.

Also, keep in mind the reality of inflation. That $0.25 cents that Martin Luther King Jr. got for each "A" when he was a child in the 1930's and 1940's would amount to about $5.00 dollars today. So if you want to pay a little more than a quarter, that's fine. You can change the increments in the incentive plan to as much or as little as you like. Just use your best judgment, and be consistent.

Next, at the end of each marking term, pay your child for his report card as follows:

A's = Pay your child $20 for each A

B's = Pay your child $10 for each B

C's = $0

D's =Your child owes you $10

F's = Your child owes you $20

Using this system, if your child brought home the following report card, here is what he or she would earn:

Subject	Grade	Amount Earned/Owed
English	A-	Child earns $20
Math	B	Child earns $10
Science	D	Child owes you $10
History	C+	Nothing earned or owed

Total Payout: $20

Your child would earn nothing for his C+ in History, he would earn $30 for his A and B in English and Math, but he owes you $10 for the D in science, so he walks away with a total of $20 that marking term.

The first time we used this incentive plan with our son, he ended up owing *me* money. I made him pay every penny. I had to, in order to empower him and get him to believe fully in the incentive plan. We had established the ground rules in the beginning that all money owed for

BIFF PRINCIPLE:

"If it ain't broke,
don't fix it."

report cards had to be paid in full before the end of the next marking period. My son had to work off his debt by doing extra chores around the house and by using some of the money he already made from his part-time job after school. Believe me, that never happened again.

Every marking term after that, he cashed in big for his hard work. The payout was well worth our investment. He ended up getting nearly a full scholarship to attend college by the end of senior year.

Again, you can change the increments in the incentive plan to as much or as little as you like. The effect is still the same. For example instead of paying $20 for an A, you may decide to pay $50 or some other amount. Just be consistent. What's important is that your child agrees that the system is fair, logical, and achievable for them with a reasonable amount of effort. It's also vitally important that your child believes you'll come through when report card time—his payday—rolls around.

A word of caution. If you have a child who is already doing well in school, you should not start giving him cash incentives for his grades. The research suggests, and we agree, that when you pay someone for something he would have already done for free, it devalues the work he was doing in the first place. In simpler terms, "If it ain't broke, don't fix it."

You can, and sometimes you must, treat different children differently. Each one of your children is different, and you shouldn't be afraid to treat them that way. Just make sure your child who's already a good student doesn't feel neglected.

For your child who is unmotivated, and failing in school, if you've tried everything else, then give cash incentives a try. We think you'll be pleasantly surprised with the results!

Best of all, gradually over time you will begin to notice that your child is bringing home good grades *not* because of the cash incentives

BIFF PRINCIPLE:

Over time, the extrinsic rewards give way to the internal motivation to do well in school.

but because of all the other things that are so much more important. That feeling of pride in his accomplishments. The satisfaction in knowing she's done her job well. The trust she has earned from you as her parents, and from her teachers in school. The admiration he receives from his friends who realize, yes your child is still cool—only now he's a cool kid with excellent grades.

Yes, over time, the extrinsic rewards give way to the internal motivation to do well in school simply for the joy of learning and being the best he can be.

We'll see
you and your child
on the Honor Roll!

These 10 tips are just a starting point for motivating your child to get A's. There are many other strategies we have learned by doing the BIFF program over the years, too many to include here in this guide-book. If you haven't already done so, please sign up for our Motivation Minute Newsletter by visiting www.student-motivation-for-better-grades.com so we can share more tips and information with you throughout the school year. We'll also let you know when a BIFF workshop will be coming to your area.

We wish you the best in motivating your child to get A's in school. We'll see you and your child on the Honor Roll!

101 Inspirational Quotes for Struggling Students

1. "We are what we repeatedly do. Excellence, therefore, is not an act but a habit." -Aristotle

2. "If you aren't going all the way, why go at all?" -Joe Namath

3. "The ability to concentrate and to use your time well is everything if you want to succeed in business--or almost anywhere else for that matter." -Lee Iacocca

4. "You can have anything you want, if you want it badly enough. You can be anything you want to be, do anything you set out to accomplish if you hold to that desire with singleness of purpose." -Abraham Lincoln

5. "The only disability in life is a bad attitude." -Scott Hamilton

6. "Minds are like parachutes - they only function when open." - Thomas Dewar

7. "Hard work truly does pay off. I started a long time ago in hopes that this day would come, where I could be recognized for my hard work." -Usher

8. "The only place where success comes before work is in the dictionary." -Vidal Sassoon

9. "People often say that motivation doesn't last. Well, neither does bathing - that's why we recommend it daily." -Zig Ziglar

10. "There is no elevator to success. You have to take the stairs." -Anonymous

11. "The beautiful thing about learning is that no one can take it away from you." -B.B King

12. "Opportunity is missed by most people because it is dressed in overalls and it looks like work." -Thomas Edison

13. "Life's real failure is when you do not realize how close you were to success when you gave up." -Unknown

14. "One important key to success is self-confidence. An important key to self-confidence is preparation." -Arthur Ashe

15. "I believe that my own success has come from a love of learning...and education was my path to possibility." -Oprah Winfrey

16. "Patience, persistence and perspiration make an unbeatable combination for success." -Napolean Hill

17. "Education is the transmission of civilization." -Ariel and Will Durant

18. "Success means having the courage, the determination, and the will to become the person you believe you were meant to be." -George Sheehan

19. "Whenever you do a thing, act as if all the world were watching." -Thomas Jefferson

20. "The aim of education should be to teach us rather how to think, than what to think - rather to improve our minds, so as to enable us to think for ourselves, than to load the memory with thoughts of other men." -Bill Beattie

21. "Great works are performed not by strength but by perseverance." - Samuel Johnson

22. "The will to win, the desire to succeed, the urge to reach your full potential… these are the keys that will unlock the door to personal excellence." -Eddie Robinson

23. "You are what you think. You are what you go for. You are what you do." -Bob Richards

24. "It's a visual thing. That's why I'm here right now, because I dreamed of these moments. Kids need that. If they don't dream, they have what?" -Britney Spears

25. "Prejudices, it is well known, are most difficult to eradicate from the heart whose soil has never been loosened or fertilized by education; they grow there, firm as weeds among rocks." -Charlotte Bronte

26. "In spite of your fear, do what you have to do." -Chin Ning Chu

27. "There are no secrets to success. It is the result of preparation, hard work, learning from failure." -Colin Powell

28. "To win without risk is to triumph without glory." -Corneille

29. "Learning is an active process. We learn by doing." -Dale Carnegie

30. "Don't bunt. Aim out of the ballpark." -David Ogilvy

31. "You will never leave where you are, until you decide where you'd rather be." -Dexter Yager

32. "Every success is built on the ability to do better than good enough." -Unknown

33. "Every day do something that will inch you closer to a better tomorrow." -Doug Firebaugh

34. "You never will be the person you can be if pressure, tension and discipline are taken out of your life." -Dr. James G. Bilkey

35. "Most of the important things in the world have been accomplished by people who have kept on trying when there seemed to be no hope at all." -Dale Carnegie

36. "Our attitude toward life determines life's attitude towards us." -Earl Nightingale

37. "The saddest failures in life are those that come from not putting forth the power and will to succeed." -Edwin Percy Welles

38. "It is better to light a candle than to curse the darkness." -Eleanor Roosevelt

39. "First say to yourself what you would be; and then do what you have to do." -Epictetus

40. "The most important thing about motivation is goal setting. You should always have a goal." -Francie Larrieu Smith

41. "A wise man will make more opportunities than he finds." -Francis Bacon

42. "You see things; and you say "Why?" But I dream things that never were; and I say "Why not?""-George Bernard Shaw

43. "Defeat is not the worst of failures. Not to have tried is the true failure." -George E. Woodberry

44. "Never let the fear of striking out get in your way." -George Herman "Babe" Ruth

45. "The aim of education is the knowledge not of fact, but of values." -Dean William R. Inge

46. "It is impossible for a man to learn what he thinks he already knows." -Epictetus

47. "You must learn day by day, year by year, to broaden your horizon. The more things you love, the more you are interested in, the more you enjoy, the more you are indignant about, the more you have left when anything happens." -Ethel Barrymore

48. "There is no happiness except in the realization that we have accomplished something." -Henry Ford

49. "A teacher affects eternity; he can never tell where his influence stops." -Henry B. Adams

50. "Go confidently in the direction of your dreams. Live the life you have imagined." -Henry David Thoreau

51. "Education makes a people easy to lead, but difficult to drive; easy to govern, but impossible to enslave." -Lord Brougham

52. "Knowledge speaks, but wisdom listens." -Jimi Hendrix

53. "Education is the most powerful weapon which you can use to change the world." -Nelson Mandela

54. "The only real mistake is the one from which we learn nothing." -John Powell

55. "Challenges are what make life interesting; overcoming them is what makes life meaningful." -Joshua J. Marine

56. "The journey of a thousand miles must begin with a single step." -Lao Tzu

57. "Apply yourself. Get all the education you can, but then, by God, do something. Don't just stand there; make it happen." -Lee Iacocca

58. "Happy are those who dream dreams and are ready to pay the price to make them come true." -Leon J. Suenes

59. "If we do not plant knowledge when young, it will give us no shade when we are old." -Lord Chesterfield

60. "I stand for freedom of expression, doing what you believe in, and going after your dreams." -Madonna

61. "You must be the change you wish to see in the world." -Mahatma Ghandi

62. "Establishing lasting peace is the work of education; all politics can do is keep us out of war." -Maria Montessori

63. "To repeat what others have said requires education; to challenge it, requires brains." -Mary Pettibone Poole

64. "You are never a loser until you quit trying." -Mike Ditka

65. "If you always do what you always did, you will always get what you always got." -Jackie "Moms" Mabley

66. "Education's purpose is to replace an empty mind with an open one." -Malcolm Forbes

67. "If what you're working for really matters, you'll give it all you've got." -Nido Qubein

68. "Natural abilities are like natural plants; they need pruning by study." -Francis Bacon

69. "If you don't go after what you want, you'll never have it. If you don't ask, the answer is always no. If you don't step forward, you're always in the same place." -Nora Roberts

70. "Develop a passion for learning. If you do, you'll never cease to grow." -Anthony J. D'Angelo

71. "The great thing in the world is not so much where we stand, as in what direction we are moving." -Oliver Wendell Holmes

72. "Learning without thought is labor lost." -Confucius

73. "Never say die." -Proverb

74. "Nothing is predestined: The obstacles of your past can become the gateways that lead to new beginnings." -Ralph Blum

75. "Do not go where the path may lead, go instead where there is no path and leave a trail." -Ralph Waldo Emerson

76. "The only thing that stands between a man and what he wants from life is often merely the will to try it and the faith to believe that it is possible." -Richard M. DeVos

77. "Where you start is not as important as where you finish." -Zig Ziglar

78. "Success is the sum of small efforts, repeated day in and day out." -Robert Collier

79. "Great works are performed not by strength but by perseverance." -Samuel Johnson

80. "Everything happens for a reason. I'm used to it, I prepare for it. Like I say, at the end of the day, those in charge of their own destiny are going to do what's rights for them." -Shaquille O'Neal

81. "Kites rise highest against the wind -- not with it." -Sir Winston Churchill

82. "Education is the ability to listen to almost anything without losing your temper or your self-confidence." -Robert Frost

83. "Genius is one percent inspiration and ninety-nine percent perspiration." -Thomas Edison

84. "There's nothing wrong with having your goals really high and trying to achieve them. That's the fun part. You may come up short. I've come up short on a lot on my goals, but it's always fun to try and achieve them." -Tiger Woods

85. "There is no knowledge that is not power." -Ralph Waldo Emerson

86. "It's easy to make a buck. It's a lot tougher to make a difference." -Tom Brokaw

87. "Know that it's your decisions, and not your conditions, that determine your destiny." -Tony Robbins

88. "What sculpture is to a block of marble, education is to the soul." -Joseph Addison

89. "The roots of education are bitter, but the fruit is sweet." -Aristotle

90. "Perseverance is not a long race, it is many short races one after another." -Walter Elliott

91. "Picture in your mind a sense of personal destiny." -Wayne Oates

92. "The main part of intellectual education is not the acquisition of facts but learning how to make facts live." -Oliver Wendell Holmes

93. "Do not depend upon teachers to educate you... follow your own bent, pursue your curiosity bravely, express yourself, make your own harmony." -Will Durant

94. "Education is not the filling of a pail, but the lighting of a fire." -William Butler Yeats

95. "If at first you don't succeed, try, try again." -William Edward Hickson

96. "The object of teaching a child is to enable him to get along without a teacher." -Elbert Hubbard

97. "Destiny is not a matter of chance, it is a matter of choice; it is not a thing to be waited for, it is a thing to be achieved." -William Jennings Bryan

98. "The direction in which education starts a man will determine his future life." -Plato

99. "The educated differ from the uneducated as much as the living from the dead." -Aristotle

100. "The only person who is educated is the one who has learned how to learn... and change." -Carl Rogers

101. "Others can stop you temporarily - you are the only one who can do it permanently." -Zig Ziglar

About the Authors

Ayele Shakur and Gary Bracey have been trailblazers in the field of motivational learning for the past decade. Since 1995, they have run the Boston Learning Center which is a nonprofit agency that provides tutoring to students in grades K-12. Together they co-created an innovative program called The BIFF Paradigm Project: A Motivational Learning Skills Program, which uses high-energy motivational methods and the latest accelerated learning techniques to motivate failing students to honor roll success. Since 1999, Gary and Ayele have taught the BIFF (*Building Inspiration From Failure*) Program to over 1,000 students in the Boston area. Gary, a native of Queens, New York and a successful entrepreneur, brings the "street smart" motivational aspects to the program while Ayele, a native of Boston, who is a Harvard-trained educator with over eleven years of classroom teaching experience, brings the "school smart" aspects to the program. Together, they are redefining what it means to be "cool in school" for kids all across America.

BIFF Millionaire Mindboost 2-Day Motivation and Study Skills Seminar

If you ever wanted your teen to take school more seriously... if you dream of getting your child to do homework without constant battles... or if you're longing to see your child with more focus and a better attitude, effort, and work habits, this event was created with you in mind.

The motivation and accelerated learning techniques you and your teen are going to learn at this 2-day event will work for anyone – both students and adults alike. This program is designed to help people of all ages learn faster, smarter, and more efficiently so that school is no longer a headache. School is fun!

So should YOU AND YOUR CHILD attend BIFF Millionaire Mindboost 2007? Here's how to tell.

If your child is:

- **In middle or high school (grades 6-12 and ages 12-18)**
- **Failing or almost failing one or more subjects**
- **Not completing homework assignments**
- **Making excuses for not doing schoolwork**
- **Suffering from a short attention span**
- **Disorganized both at home and at school**
- **Lacking confidence in his own academic ability**
- **Complaining that school is too hard**
- **In danger of having to attend summer school**
- **In danger of having to repeat the current grade**

And You as a parent:

- **Are anxious about your child's future** – and you want to make sure your child gets back on the right track.
- Want to know how to **instantly shift your child's attitude**, and improve his effort and work habits so he can rise to the top.
- **Want the secrets to making homework time a snap**, so that it's easier, and less time-consuming than ever before, using the latest accelerated learning methods and technology.
- **Want the "big picture strategy"** for how to succeed as a master motivator at home.
- **Crave the secrets of using powerful incentives** that can create "the positive attitude" your child needs.
- **Have questions** about things to try or do at home to keep your child motivated throughout the school year from September through June.
- Want to learn how to **leverage academic resources** such as college counseling, diagnostic testing, and high-impact, high-quality, professional tutoring free of charge using proven, simple methods.
- **Want to know the secrets of promoting** better grades…so you can leave the worrying and arguments in the dust forever.

… yes, BIFF Millionaire Mindboost is THE event for You and your Child!

BIFF Millionaire Mindboost will load your teen up with tons of insightful, innovative strategies and tactics that empower him to read, memorize, take notes, and study faster by thinking of school as a game he can win.

Here's what students are saying…

"BIFF Millionaire Mindboost has finally shown me that doing well in school is possible and that all I need is to change what I do. BIFF has given me hope that I will improve and that there are other ways of improving than the ones I have been taught before. Thank you, BIFF Millionaire Mindboost. I can do better!"

"When I was signed up for the program, I thought I had just lost a whole weekend. But in truth, the program is a lot of fun, and the tips and tricks discussed seem legit. It's a great program. My only regret is not knowing about it earlier."

"Absolutely loved the program."

'BIFF Millionaire Mindboost is a very good experience. It has motivated me in many ways. It has shown me many different ways to study and how to be successful in life."

Here's what parents are saying…

"I enjoyed the different strategies and resources to assist my child in school, which also were very helpful for myself."

"I really enjoyed the workshop and there were a lot of strategies to use. All of the strategies made a lot of sense and I will be more than happy to put them to the test."

"I thought the instructors were very good at what they presented. They seem to know what every child needs to be successful."

To register, visit <u>http://www.student-motivation-for-better-grades.com</u> and click on Events.

APPENDIX

A Special Report: What Your Teen Doesn't Want You to Know About the Student Motivation Crisis in American Schools

Some very savvy students in some not so savvy public schools have figured out that if a school doesn't have their correct parent contact information, there is no way for the school to get in touch with their parents – no matter how outrageously disruptive they may be. If the child has recently moved and the parents have not given the school administrators their new address and phone number because they assume their child did, this child is given free reign to wreak havoc in the classroom and school hallways.

In his most recent book, *High School Confidential: Secrets of an Undercover Student*, twenty-four year old author Jeremy Iversen went deep undercover posing as a teenager at a suburban high school in Southern California. What he found there was a fast-paced world of "promiscuous freshmen girls, lunchtime alcoholics and perfectionist drug dealers," with rampant recreational drug use, sexual escapades, and apathetic teachers who didn't even bother to teach.

These two examples are symptoms of a much larger issue – the growing crisis of low motivation in American schools. Many students, with good reason, have become turned off by school and see it as more of a social playground than an institution of learning.

Most of us can remember our adolescent years. Being a teenager meant more freedom, more possibilities, and much to our surprise more responsibility. School work became harder, our parents always seemed to be unhappy with what we did no matter how hard we tried. The teenage years were difficult for many and downright awful for some. But today you are a parent, and you probably already recognize that in many ways teenagers today are different from teenagers back in your time.

How Unmotivated Are Students Today When it Comes to School?

- ❖ 60% of teenagers admitted they could do much better in school if they tried

- ❖ 50% of students do not work up to their academic potential because they are indifferent about academic performance and more interested in sports and social activities

- ❖ 50% said their schools do not challenge them enough to do their best

- ❖ Less than 50% reported taking their studies seriously

- ❖ 80% disagreed with the statement that it is important to get good grades in school.[ii]

"Motivation is essential to learning at all ages, but it becomes pivotal during adolescence as youth approach the threshold to adulthood." - Engaging Schools

If you are struggling with an unmotivated teenager who is failing in school or bringing home mediocre grades you are not alone. Many teenagers all across America from the cities to the suburbs are unmotivated and disengaged when it comes to school. They fail classes, attend summer school, barely study, don't do homework – and worst of all, they don't seem to care.

The Truth About this Rising Crisis:
No, It's Not Just Normal Adolescence

No, it's not your imagination. It's part of a growing epidemic – a rising crisis of low motivation and underachievement in American schools. You may find it difficult to believe that in this day and age of high standards and high stakes tests, student motivation is actually on the decline. But it's true.

Teens today have a lot of different activities and distractions competing for their attention, and pulling their focus away from school. About 40% of all teens have part-time jobs after school. Teens spend an average of two hours a day hanging out with friends and another three hours watching television each day.

Low academic motivation creeps in around fourth grade and grows steadily worse through middle school and high school. By high school, many students have psychologically dropped out and some have physically dropped out as well. At this pivotal age, most adolescents are too old to blindly follow the demands of their teachers yet too young to fully appreciate the important role that school plays in their future success. So school becomes a waste of time.

**"The steady decrease
in school engagement and motivation to learn
that occurs as students progress from the early grades, through
middle school, and into high school, and corresponding drop in the
ranking of U.S. students relative to their international counterparts
in standardized measures of learning, strongly suggest that something is seriously wrong with American high schools."
- Engaging Schools**

For those students reaching college, the picture is just as bleak. One survey conducted by *Money Magazine* found that college students "are less engaged with school now than they were 20 years ago" and another report from the Educational Research Service found that "the percentage of college freshman who report they talked with teachers outside of class, studied more than six hours a week, or belonged to student clubs has been declining over the past 10 years." [iii]

If academic motivation is on the decline for even college kids, our best and brightest, then it's time to recognize that this is a serious issue in America. Learning is as natural a human instinct as eating and breathing. All humans have a natural curiosity, a burning need to ask questions, a need to make sense of their world, to explore new things, and solve new problems. All students are motivated to learn. But over the past twenty years, there have been forces at work in society, forces that are right in front of your eyes that you probably haven't thought about, that are stripping away students' motivation to excel in school.

In 1983, a controversial report issued by the Department of Education called A *Nation at Risk*, shined a spotlight on the danger of America falling behind other countries and losing the power it has held for so long as a leader in innovation and technology. This report ushered in slow but steady and dramatic changes in education reform and set the stage for political battles over how to educate America's children.

Despite 25 years of education reform efforts, there is still very little improvement in the nation's overall scores on national measures of academic achievement. Today we have the ambitious No Child Left Behind Act which was signed into law by President Bush in 2001 to ensure that all children become proficient in reading, writing, and math by the year 2014. Now all across America, millions of dollars are being poured into after-school tutoring, teacher training, school restructuring, imaginative new curricula, building renovations, and the list goes on and on. But all of these worthy efforts will only succeed to the extent that the students themselves are motivated and willing to learn.

"As long as such a significant proportion of students are either indifferent to school or alienated from it, it is not surprising that efforts at school reform have not yielded greater results.

- Engaging Schools

As a parent, if your punishment and reward system isn't working, and you're constantly being called up to your teen's school for meetings with her teachers, and each report card is another disaster, and you don't seem to be able to get through to your child, it's not because of your parenting skills. It's a much deeper, pervasive issue that parents all across America are struggling with.

When you start attacking the issue from the standpoint that your teen is part of a larger epidemic, you can equip yourself with real tools and techniques to combat the problem and get your child back on track.

Early Warning Signs That Your Child is Becoming a Statistic in the Low Motivation Crisis

You can look at student motivation from 3 different vantage points:

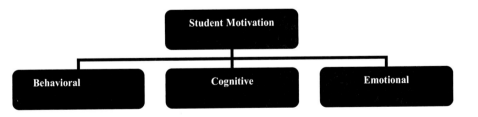

BEHAVIORAL: Is your child attending school regularly, or is she skipping classes and repeatedly absent? Is she completing homework assignments on time, or losing assignments on a regular basis? Do you have to constantly nag your child to do her homework, or to get up in the morning to go to school? Does she proactively seek out her teachers to get extra help when she needs it, or does she fall asleep at the back of the room letting the day's lesson pass her by?

COGNITIVE: Does your child put forth the effort to learn and apply new concepts? Does he study and review necessary materials? Does he ask for help when he doesn't understand something? Does he give up easily when the work is too hard?

EMOTIONAL: Does your child show enthusiasm for learning new things? Does he take pride in his work? Does he enjoy school? Is he socially well adjusted with a group of dependable friends at school that he feels connected to?

◙

These are some of the signs of a teen with a healthy level of motivation when it comes to school. Occasional battles over homework time, priority setting, and school performance are normal. But when these discussions become heated, nightly battles, there may be something deeper going on. Your child may be headed for or already in a dangerous, motivational slump. It's time to get help.

*Reference:

National Research Council and Institute of Medicine. (2004). *Engaging Schools: Fostering High School Students' Motivation to Learn.* Committee on Increasing High School Students' Engagement and Motivation to Learn. Board on Children, Youth, and Families, Division of Behavioral and Social Sciences and Education. Washington, DC. The National Academies Press.

Student Motivation Survey
for Parents

This survey is designed to help you identify your child's student motivation quotient on a scale of 1-100. For best results, have your child also take the Student Motivation Survey Self-Assessment. You will rate all of the statements on a scale of 1-5, with 5 being highest. Take your time and give honest answers.

My child is very well organized.

Less True - 1 ☐ 2 ☐ 3 ☐ 4 ☐ 5 ☐ - More True

My child has good work habits and study habits.

Less True - 1 ☐ 2 ☐ 3 ☐ 4 ☐ 5 ☐ - More True

My child has never had a violent outburst or gotten into a fight at school.

Less True - 1 ☐ 2 ☐ 3 ☐ 4 ☐ 5 ☐ - More True

My child is working up to his full potential.

Less True - 1 ☐ 2 ☐ 3 ☐ 4 ☐ 5 ☐ - More True

My child does NOT let his friends distract him from doing his schoolwork and homework.

Less True - 1 ☐ 2 ☐ 3 ☐ 4 ☐ 5 ☐ - More True

My child always does his homework without me having to remind him.

Less True - 1 ☐ 2 ☐ 3 ☐ 4 ☐ 5 ☐ - More True

My child has never been diagnosed with Attention-Deficit-Disorder (ADD).

Less True - 1 ☐ 2 ☐ 3 ☐ 4 ☐ 5 ☐ - More True

My child likes to put a lot of thought and effort into his work.

Less True - 1 ☐ 2 ☐ 3 ☐ 4 ☐ 5 ☐ - More True

My child has never repeated a grade in middle or high school (grades 6-12).

Less True - 1 ☐ 2 ☐ 3 ☐ 4 ☐ 5 ☐ - More True

My child would rather be seen as 'school smart' than 'street smart.'

Less True - 1 ☐ 2 ☐ 3 ☐ 4 ☐ 5 ☐ - More True

My child wakes up in the morning refreshed and ready for school.

Less True - 1 ☐ 2 ☐ 3 ☐ 4 ☐ 5 ☐ - More True

My child rarely complains about school.

Less True - 1 ☐ 2 ☐ 3 ☐ 4 ☐ 5 ☐ - More True

My child works hard in school even when he doesn't like the teacher.

Less True - 1 ☐ 2 ☐ 3 ☐ 4 ☐ 5 ☐ - More True

My child has a positive attitude and positive beliefs about school.

Less True - 1 ☐ 2 ☐ 3 ☐ 4 ☐ 5 ☐ - More True

In the past two years, my child has never been suspended from school.

Less True - 1 ☐ 2 ☐ 3 ☐ 4 ☐ 5 ☐ - More True

My child has never been expelled from school for his behavior.

Less True - 1 ☐ 2 ☐ 3 ☐ 4 ☐ 5 ☐ - More True

My child does NOT have an Individualized Education Plan (IEP) for special needs students.

Less True - 1 ☐ 2 ☐ 3 ☐ 4 ☐ 5 ☐ - More True

On his last report card, my child had A's and B's in all of his classes.

Less True - 1 ☐ 2 ☐ 3 ☐ 4 ☐ 5 ☐ - More True

Over the past two years, my child has never attended mandatory summer school for a failing grade.

Less True - 1 ☐ 2 ☐ 3 ☐ 4 ☐ 5 ☐ - More True

If I had the opportunity to get a FREE 30-minute consultation with a certified motivational learning skills expert who could help my child become more motivated with better grades in school, I would definitely sign up.

Less True - 1 ☐ 2 ☐ 3 ☐ 4 ☐ 5 ☐ - More True

Get Score

Note: Our most recent, updated, and revised surveys are available on the web at www.student-motivation-for-better-grades.com.

Student Motivation Survey
Self-Assessment (for Students)

This survey is designed to help you identify your student motivation quotient on a scale of 1-100. You will rate all of the statements on a scale of 1-5, with 5 being highest. Take your time and give honest answers.

I am very well organized.

Less True - 1 ☐ 2 ☐ 3 ☐ 4 ☐ 5 ☐ - More True

I have good work habits and study habits.

Less True - 1 ☐ 2 ☐ 3 ☐ 4 ☐ 5 ☐ - More True

I have never had a violent outburst or gotten into a fight at school.

Less True - 1 ☐ 2 ☐ 3 ☐ 4 ☐ 5 ☐ - More True

I feel I am working up to my full potential.

Less True - 1 ☐ 2 ☐ 3 ☐ 4 ☐ 5 ☐ - More True

I don't let my friends distract me from doing my schoolwork and homework.

Less True - 1 ☐ 2 ☐ 3 ☐ 4 ☐ 5 ☐ - More True

I always do my homework without my parents or teachers having to remind me.

Less True - 1 ☐ 2 ☐ 3 ☐ 4 ☐ 5 ☐ - More True

I have never been diagnosed with Attention-Deficit-Disorder (ADD).

Less True - 1 ☐ 2 ☐ 3 ☐ 4 ☐ 5 ☐ - More True

I like to put a lot of thought and effort into my work.

Less True - 1 ☐ 2 ☐ 3 ☐ 4 ☐ 5 ☐ - More True

I have never repeated a grade in middle or high school (grades 6-12).

Less True - 1 ☐ 2 ☐ 3 ☐ 4 ☐ 5 ☐ - More True

I would rather be seen as 'school smart' than 'street smart.'

Less True - 1 ☐ 2 ☐ 3 ☐ 4 ☐ 5 ☐ - More True

I wake up in the morning feeling refreshed and ready for school.

Less True - 1 ☐ 2 ☐ 3 ☐ 4 ☐ 5 ☐ - More True

I rarely complain about school.

Less True - 1 ☐ 2 ☐ 3 ☐ 4 ☐ 5 ☐ - More True

I work hard in school even when I don't like the teacher.

Less True - 1 ☐ 2 ☐ 3 ☐ 4 ☐ 5 ☐ - More True

I have a positive attitude and positive beliefs about school.

Less True - 1 ☐ 2 ☐ 3 ☐ 4 ☐ 5 ☐ - More True

In the past two years, I have never been suspended from school.

Less True - 1 ☐ 2 ☐ 3 ☐ 4 ☐ 5 ☐ - More True

I have never been expelled from school for my behavior.

Less True - 1 ☐ 2 ☐ 3 ☐ 4 ☐ 5 ☐ - More True

I do NOT have an Individualized Education Plan (IEP) for special needs students.

Less True - 1 ☐ 2 ☐ 3 ☐ 4 ☐ 5 ☐ - More True

On my last report card, I had A's and B's in all of my classes.

Less True - 1 ☐ 2 ☐ 3 ☐ 4 ☐ 5 ☐ - More True

Over the past two years, I have never attended mandatory summer school for a failing grade.

Less True - 1 ☐ 2 ☐ 3 ☐ 4 ☐ 5 ☐ - More True

If I had the opportunity to get a FREE 30-minute consultation with a certified motivational learning skills expert who could help me become more motivated with better grades in school, I would definitely sign up.

Less True - 1 ☐ 2 ☐ 3 ☐ 4 ☐ 5 ☐ - More True

Get Score

Note: Our most recent, updated, and revised surveys are available on the web at www.student-motivation-for-better-grades.com.

Tell a Friend About Stop Flunking!

Dear Readers,

If you enjoyed *Stop Flunking! A Guide for Parents: How to Motivate Your Child to Get A's in School*, then encourage your friends, school, after-school program, church, synagogue, or community center to order a copy as well.

Tell them to visit: www.stopflunking.com for ordering information.

Or use this link for easy referrals:

http://www.stopflunking.com/referrals.php

Motivation Minute Newsletter

Sign up for our *Motivation Minute Newsletter* designed to help busy parents and educators learn innovative ways to motivate middle and high school students. Twice each month, we bring you featured articles, special offers, motivation tips, and free downloads all designed to help students get mega-motivated, and succeed in school.

We know you are busy, so we promise to keep our newsletter short enough to read in just minutes, yet power-packed with information. Plus, we'll let you know when BIFF will be coming to your city or town! Go to www.student-motivation-for-better-grades.com to sign up today.

Bibliography

Endnotes

[i] Anthony P. Carnevale and Donna M. Desrochers, *Standards for What? The Economic Roots of K-16 Reform* (Washington DC: Educational Testing Service, 2003).

[ii] Public Agenda Survey, 1997, as cited in *Engaging Schools (2004).*

[iii] Gerald W. Bracey, *Setting the Record Straight: Responses to the Misconceptions About Public Education in the United States* (Alexandria, Virginia: Association for Supervision and Curriculum Development, 1997).

References

National Research Council and the Institute of Medicine. *Engaging Schools: Fostering High School Students' Motivation to Learn.* Board on Children, Youth, and Families, Division of Behavioral and Social Sciences and Education. Washington, DC: The National Academies Press. (2004).

James Comer, MD, *Leave No Child Behind: Preparing Today's Youth for Tomorrow's World* (New Haven: Yale University Press, 2004).

Gary Orfield, *Dropouts in America* (Cambridge: Harvard University Press, 2004).

Contact Us

We love hearing from our readers! If you have any questions or comments about *Stop Flunking! A Guide for Parents: How to Motivate Your Child To Get A's in School*, or if you want to learn more about The BIFF Program, feel free to contact us:

Motivational Learning Skills, Inc.
208 Ashmont Street
Boston, MA 02124
1-800-981-5535
contactauthors@stopflunking.com